A JOURNEY AROUND LIMERICKS

Limericks by Fergus Dignan

Cartoons by Peter Westley

First published in 2018 by Tawny Barn Books

Copyright © Fergus Dignan 2018

Copyright © Peter Westley 2018

The right of Fergus Dignan to be identified as the author and the right of Peter Westley to be identified as the cartoonist of this book have been asserted by them in accordance with the Copyright, Designs and Patents Act, 1988.

This book is sold subject to the condition that it shall not, by way of trade or otherwise, be lent, resold, hired out or otherwise circulated without the publisher's prior consent in any form of binding or cover other than that in which it is published and without a similar condition including this condition being imposed on the subsequent purchaser.

ISBN 978-1-9996728-0-5

CONTENTS

Map of Ireland

Foreword

Limericks 1-30:

1.	County Kerry
2.	Slea Head
3-4.	Tralee
5.	County Clare
6.	Ennis
7.	Gort
8.	Athlone
9.	County Mayo
10.	County Fermanagh
11-12.	County Donegal
13.	Strabane
14.	County Tyrone
15.	Larne
16-17.	County Armagh
18.	County Down
19.	Kilkeel
20.	Dundalk
21.	Naas

22. Kildare
23. County Offaly
24. Kilkenny
25. Rosslare
26. Tramore
27. Cork
28. Kinsale
29-30. Skibbereen

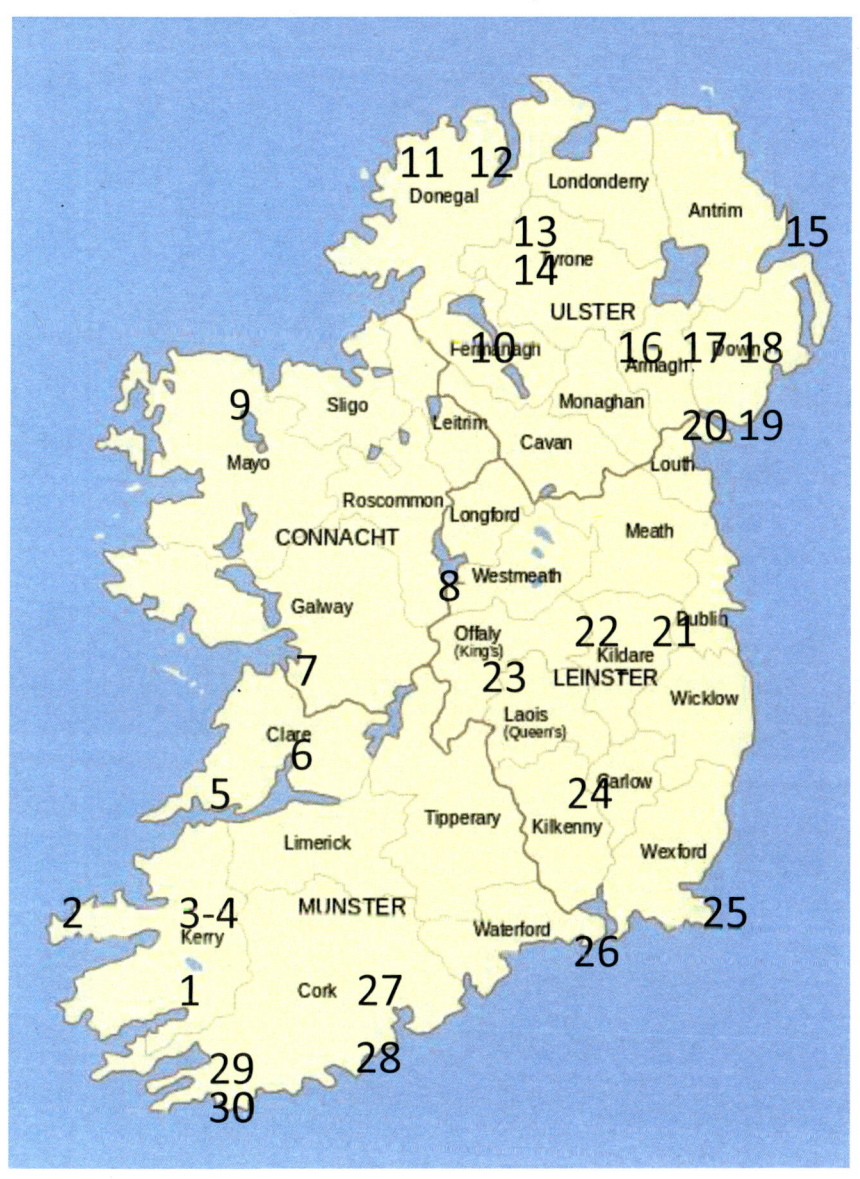

Map of Ireland

The numbers refer to the location of each limerick in the book.

FOREWORD

A limerick is a poem of five lines, and in general, has the following characteristics: lines one, two and five rhyme with each other, each having seven to ten syllables. Lines three and four rhyme and have five to six syllables each.

However, sticking rigidly to syllable numbers has the potential to affect the cadence of the limerick, so I have used these numbers as guidance only.

The origin of the word 'limerick' is not definitively known, but one of the more common theories is as follows:

There was a popular song amongst Irish soldiers in the 1890s which had the refrain:

"Won't you come up to Limerick?"

The verses were generally bawdy and humorous and made up spontaneously. The song and the poetry style as described above became

conflated and the word *limerick* came into common usage to describe such poetry.
The first evidence of limerick-style poetry (but with no lewd connotations!) was written in the form of a Latin prayer by Thomas Aquinas. Limericks were also written by William Shakespeare, examples of which can be found in *King Lear*, *Othello* and *The Tempest*. Edward Lear wrote *A Book of Nonsense* in 1846 which contained 72 limericks. Of note, the last word in the first and fifth lines was often the same.

Other than the rules that I have described in the first paragraph, limericks don't have to be about places, Irish or otherwise, nor do they have to be vulgar. Nevertheless, in writing this small book of limericks I decided to confine myself to Irish place and county names only, in recognition of the limerick's roots. In order to appeal to as wide an audience as possible, including children, I have resisted bawdiness, although there were minor outbreaks of lewdness in the poems involving Clare and Donegal!

Incidentally, I have not written a limerick about Limerick because I couldn't come up with one that would do the place name justice. I am sure that the reader will agree that Limerick isn't the most rhyming of words!

Please follow the map of Ireland to view the sites of the location names. I have numbered the limericks in a clockwise direction, starting at County Kerry in the south-west corner of the Republic of Ireland.

Fergus Dignan

There was a young man from Kerry

who captained a cross-channel ferry.

When hitting the bottle

he'd push down the throttle

and the trip would get quite scary.

Limerick 1

A silly old man from Slea Head

built a cliff-edge garden shed.

The wind he'd forgotten

so was blown to the bottom

and the gulls on his body they fed.

Limerick 2

There was an old man from Tralee

who possessed many a key.

People thought it odd

'cause the silly old sod

had no car and lived in a tree.

Limerick 3

There was a young lady from Tralee

who'd read your palm for a fee.

If the news was bad

she appeared quite sad

but actually was bursting with glee.

Limerick 4

There was an old man from Clare

who jumped over a hedge for a dare.

But the top he did hit,

falling arse over tit,

with his bum pointing up in the air.

Limerick 5

A lively old lady from Ennis

was exceptionally good at lawn tennis.

She cut a fine dash

with her cross-court smash

and pink pantaloons from Venice.

Limerick 6

There was an old lady from Gort

on whose nose grew a very long wart.

The sight of her snout

brought the birdies out

and around her nose they'd cavort.

Limerick 7

A young woman from Athlone

was never off the phone.

Her endless chatter

was no laughing matter:

by her spouse the door she was shown.

Limerick 8

There was an old lady from Mayo

who got stronger by the day-o.

She packed a big punch

so when served a duff lunch

the waiter was floored by a KO.

Limerick 9

There was a hot-tempered young man from Fermanagh

who'd clean your car for a tanner.

For clients not content

aerials would be bent

and windscreens smashed with a spanner.

Limerick 10

There was an old man from Donegal

who got an invite to a ball.

But the floor was cleared

as the old man appeared,

dancing naked except for a shawl.

Limerick 11

There was an old lady from Donegal,

often in church she would fall.

One day the vicar

lost it and hit her-

she left in a coffin, I recall.

Limerick 12

There was a handsome young man from Strabane

who was offered the part of best man.

He forgot the ring

but the real sting

was driving off with the bride in his van.

Limerick 13

There was an old man from Tyrone

who gave a dog a bone.

It had him for seconds

or so it is reckoned

as his location remains unknown.

Limerick 14

There was an old farmer from Larne

who had one very long arm.

When he rang the door bell

it was difficult to tell

whether outside or back at his farm.

Limerick 15

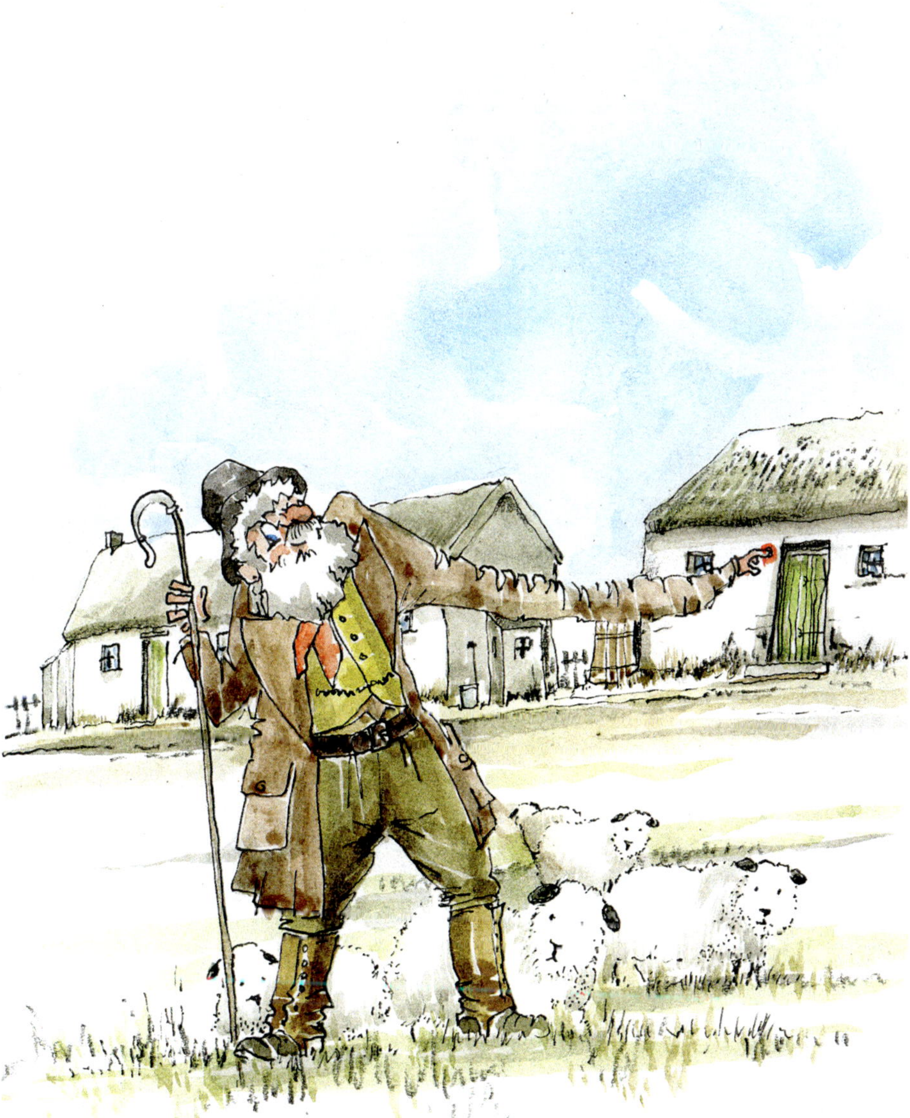

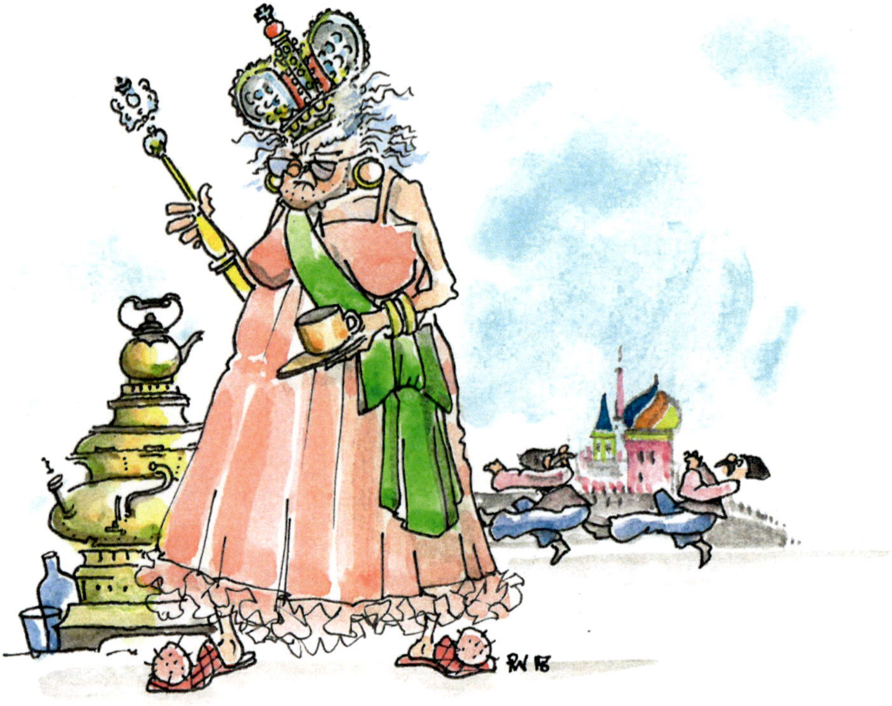

There was an old lady from Armagh

who thought that she was a czar.

She spoke fluent Russian

in any discussion

and drank tea from a samovar.

Limerick 16

There was an old man from Armagh

who never said thank you or ta.

He was especially ungrateful

when given a plateful

of sliced lemons mixed with catarrh.

Limerick 17

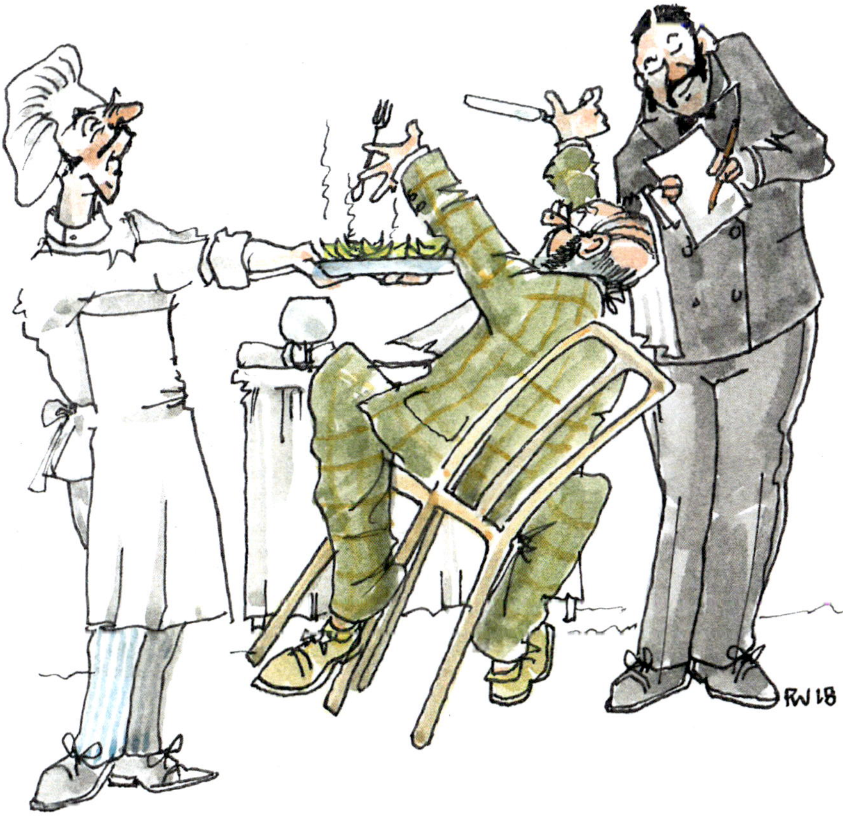
RW 18

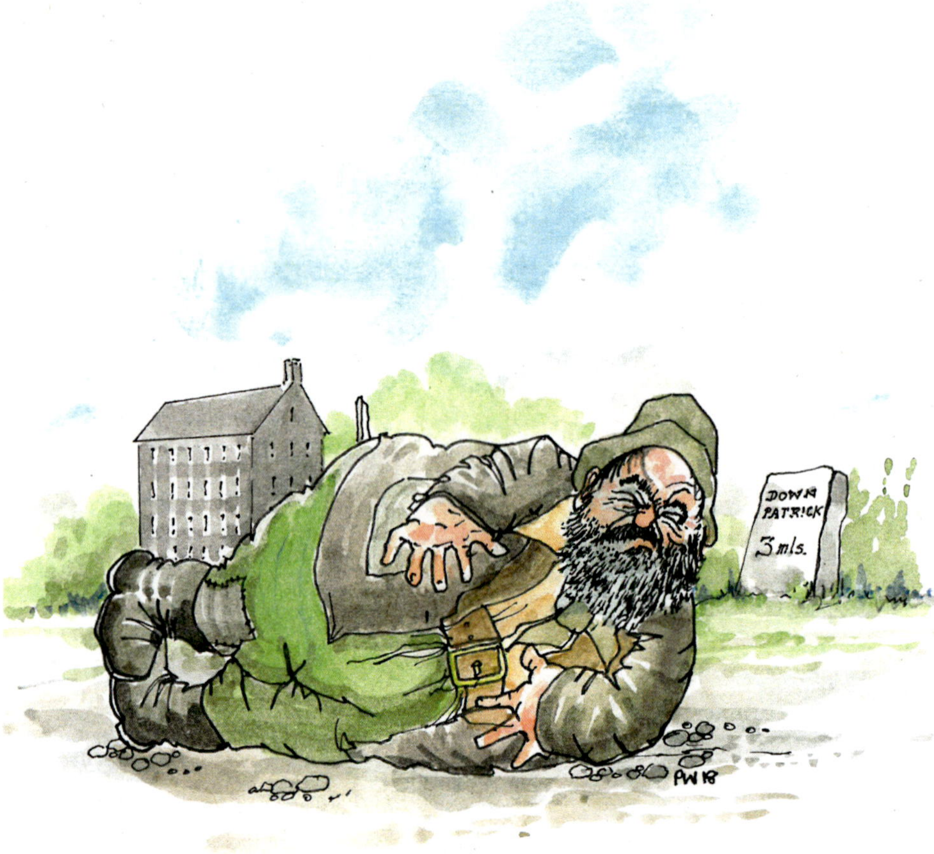
DOWN PATRICK
3 mls.
PW 18

There was an old man from County Down

who was fat and exceptionally round.

One day when not sober

he swayed, falling over

and rolled many miles out of town.

Limerick 18

There was an old man from Kilkeel

who regurgitated every meal.

The sight on the table

made his wife unstable

and on to the floor she'd reel.

Limerick 19

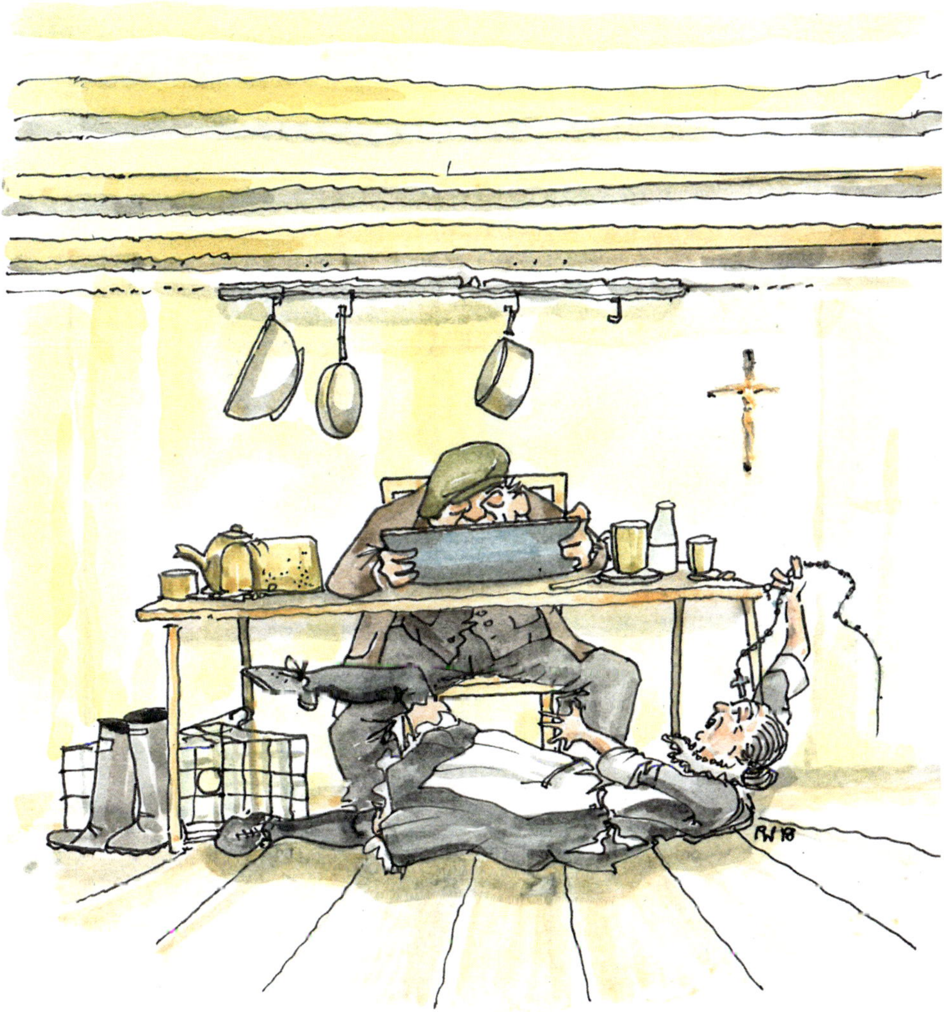

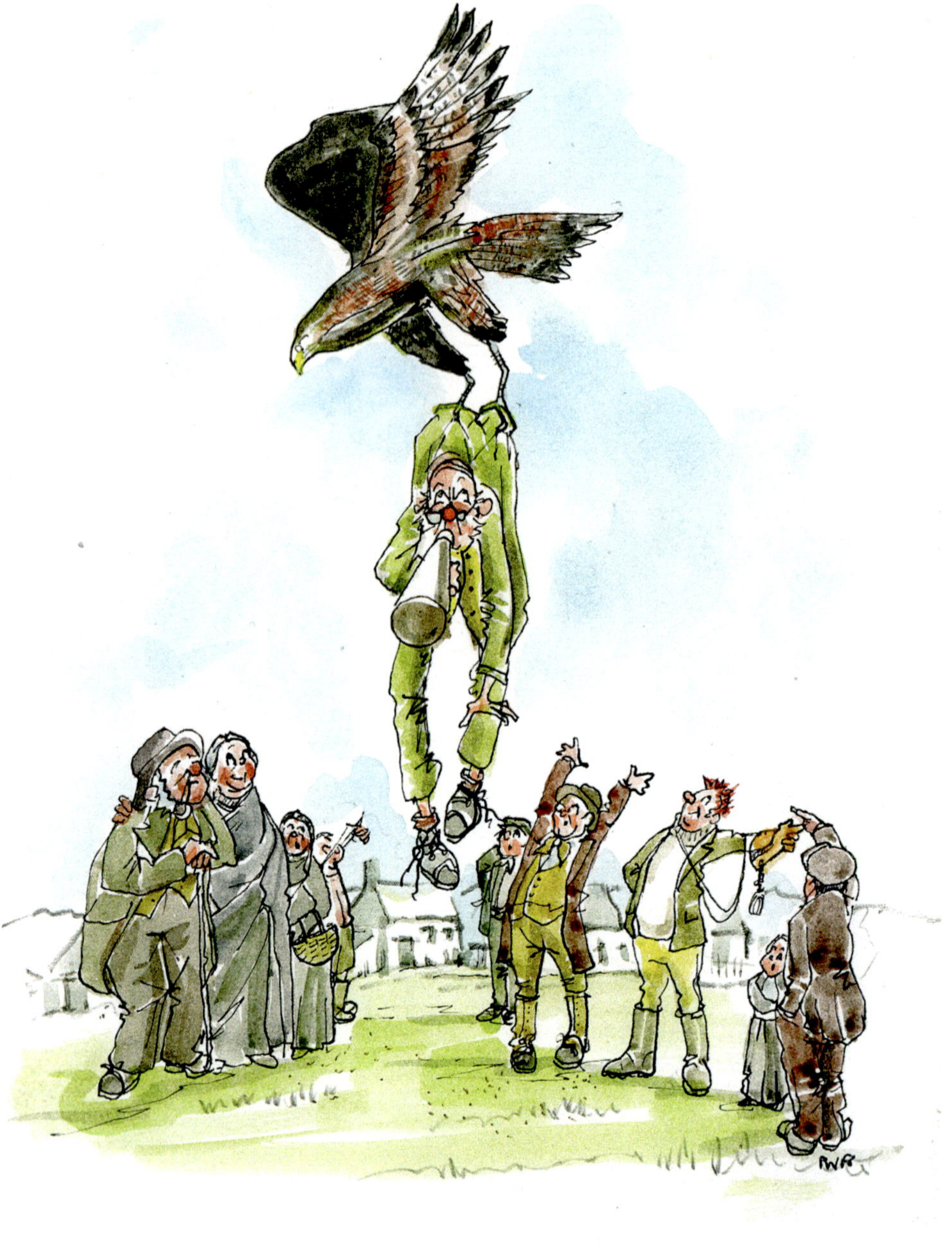

There was an old man from Dundalk

who barely drew breath for the talk.

The town grew very tired

so a falconer was hired

and he was carried away by a hawk.

Limerick 20

There was an old nag from Naas

that could never win a race.

Until chilli was inserted

in a place that it hurted

and now he gallops apace.

Limerick 21

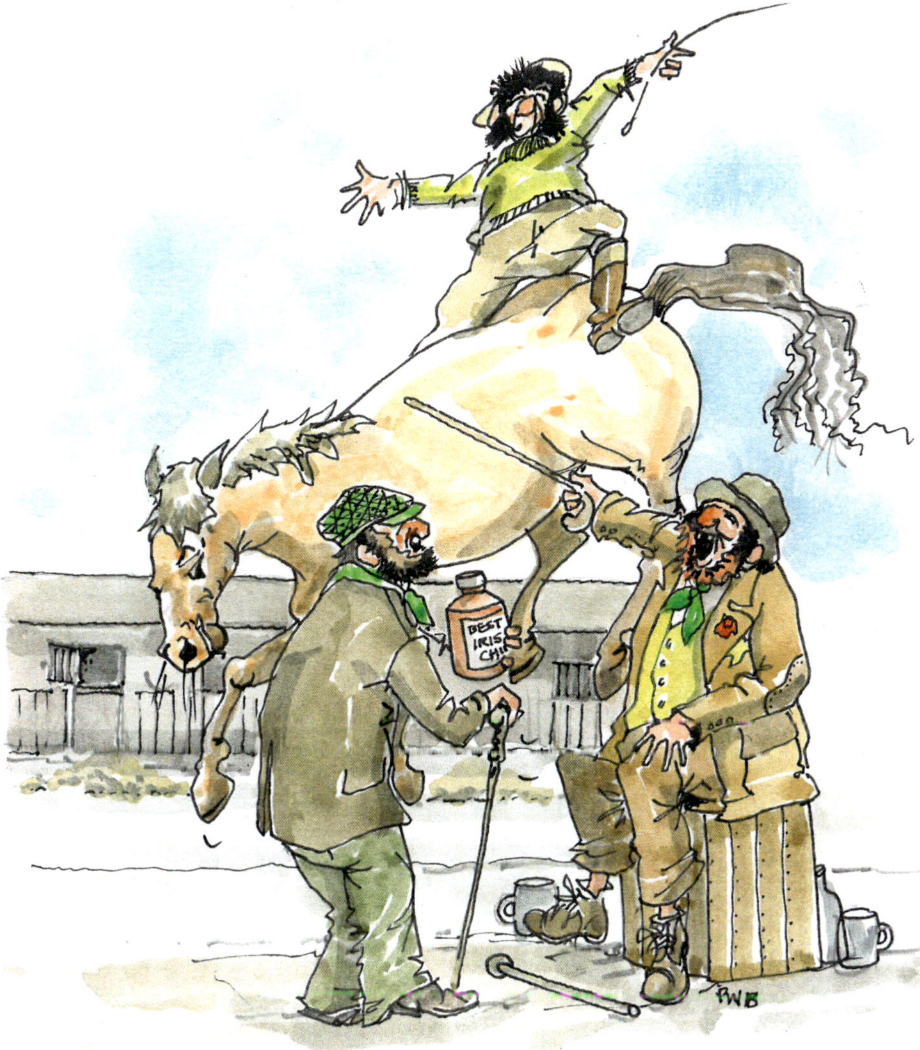
BEST
IRIS
CHI
RWB

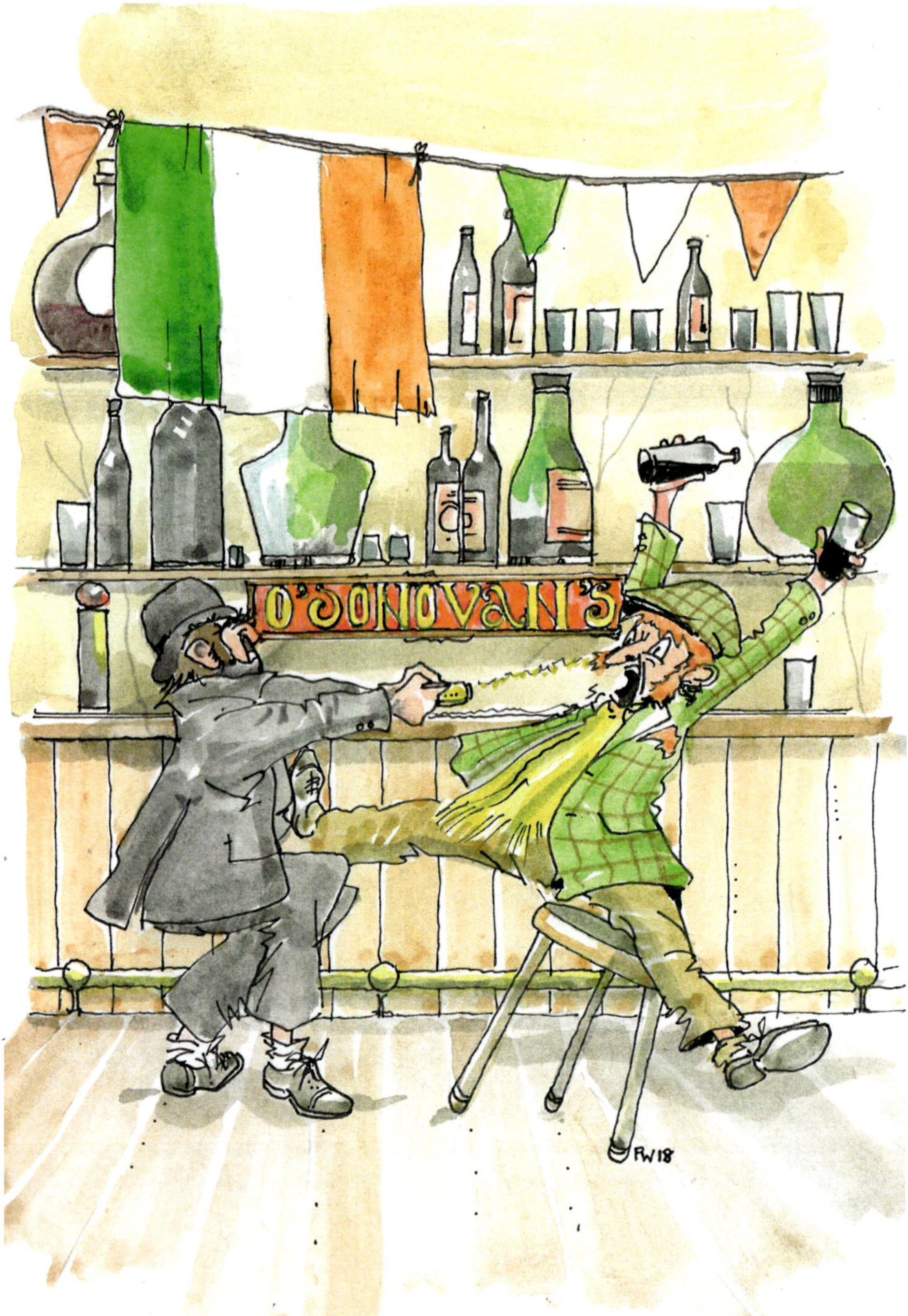
O'SONOVAN'S
RW18

There was an old man from Kildare

who had a peculiar stare.

His eyes were like lasers

'til I took out my tazers

and toasted them medium rare.

Limerick 22

There was a grand old man of Offaly

who spoke frightfully awfully.

He got in a huff

when told " that's enough!"

and shot the whinger unlawfully.

Limerick 23

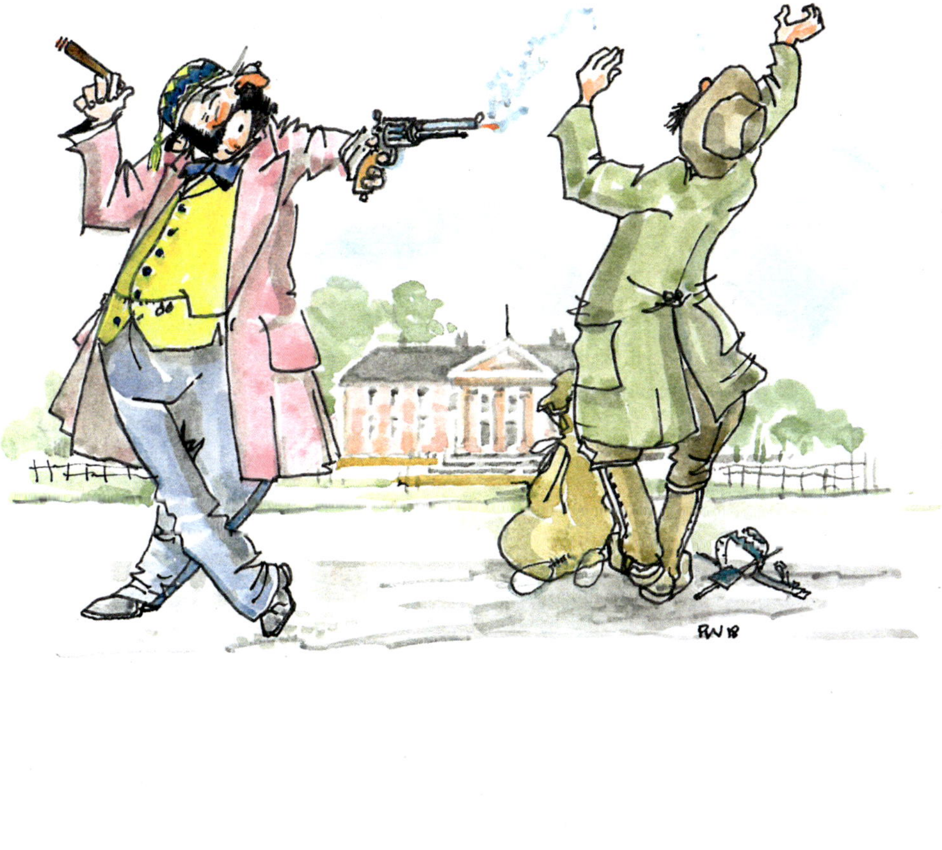

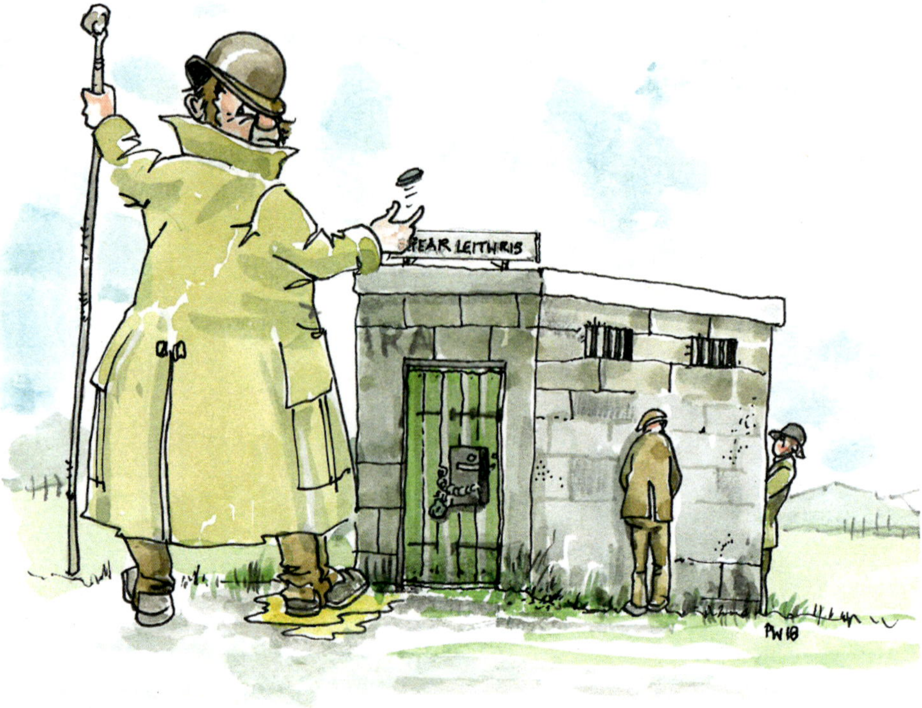
FEAR LEITHRIS
IRA
PW 18

There was an old man from Kilkenny

who rarely spent a penny.

Then feeling discommoded

his huge bladder exploded

and now a penny he spends many.

Limerick 24

There was a young man from Rosslare,

who attached four balloons to his chair.

He got a big fright

when he rose to great height

and finally landed in Clare.

Limerick 25

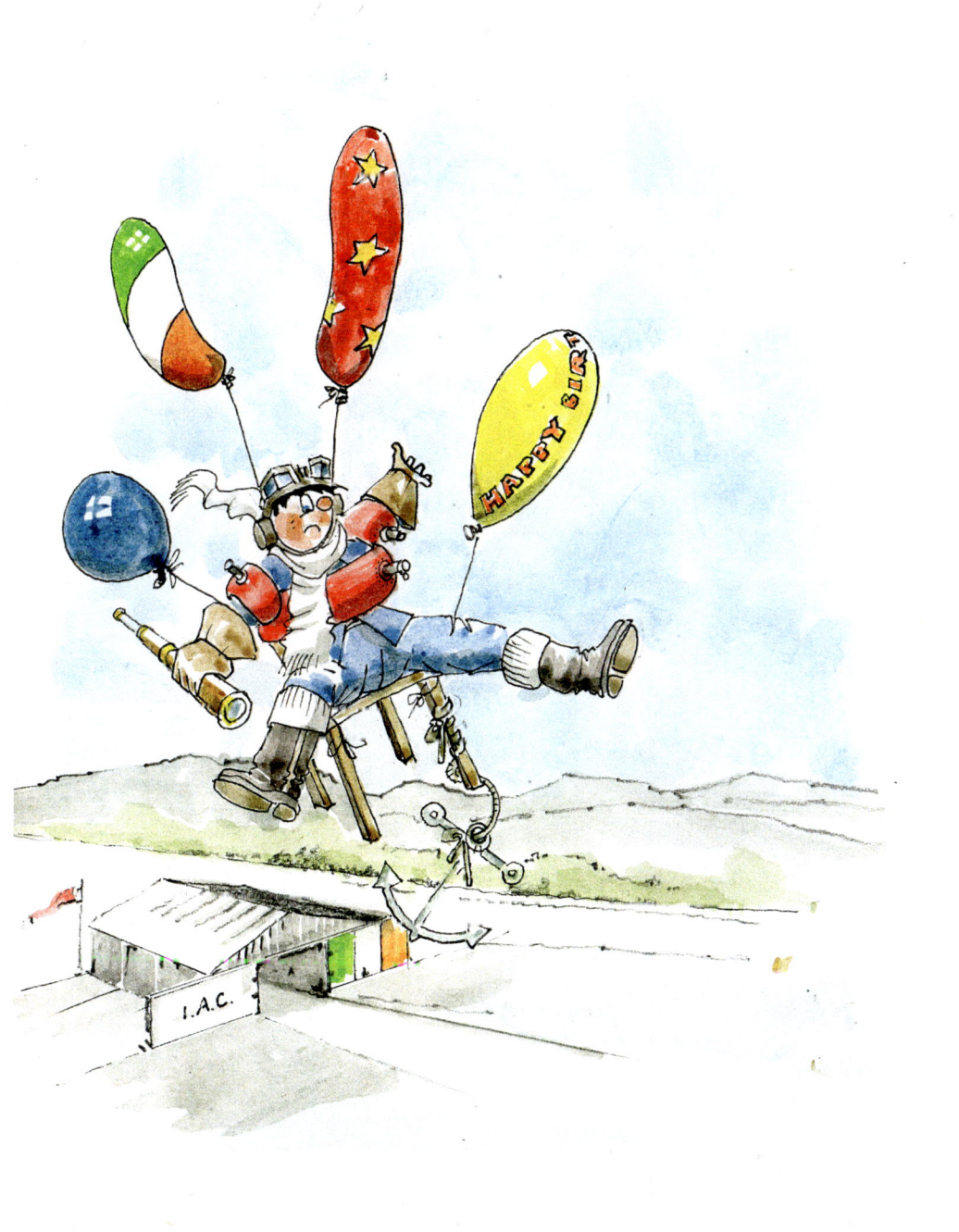
HAPPY BIRT
I.A.C.

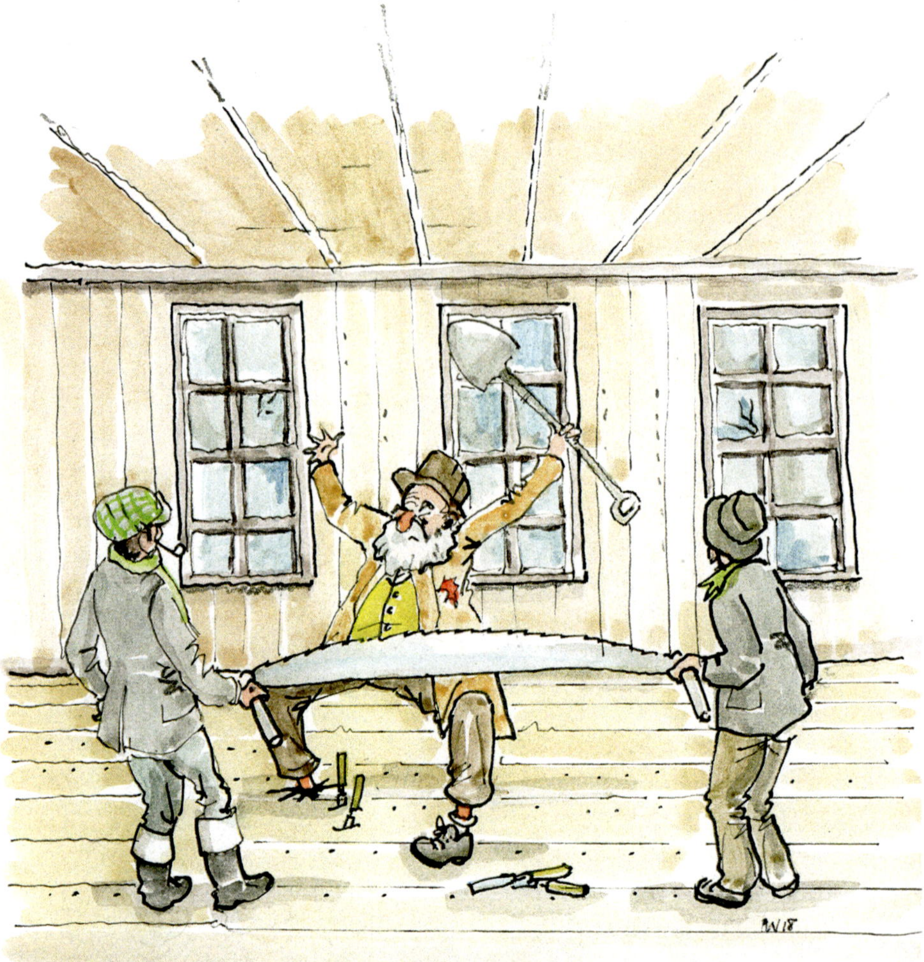

There was an old man from Tramore

whose foot got stuck in the floor.

No difference was made

using chisel or spade

so off came his leg with a saw.

Limerick 26

There was a grand old lady of Cork

who never ate with a fork.

She paid with her life

when she swallowed a knife

whilst downing a large piece of pork.

Limerick 27

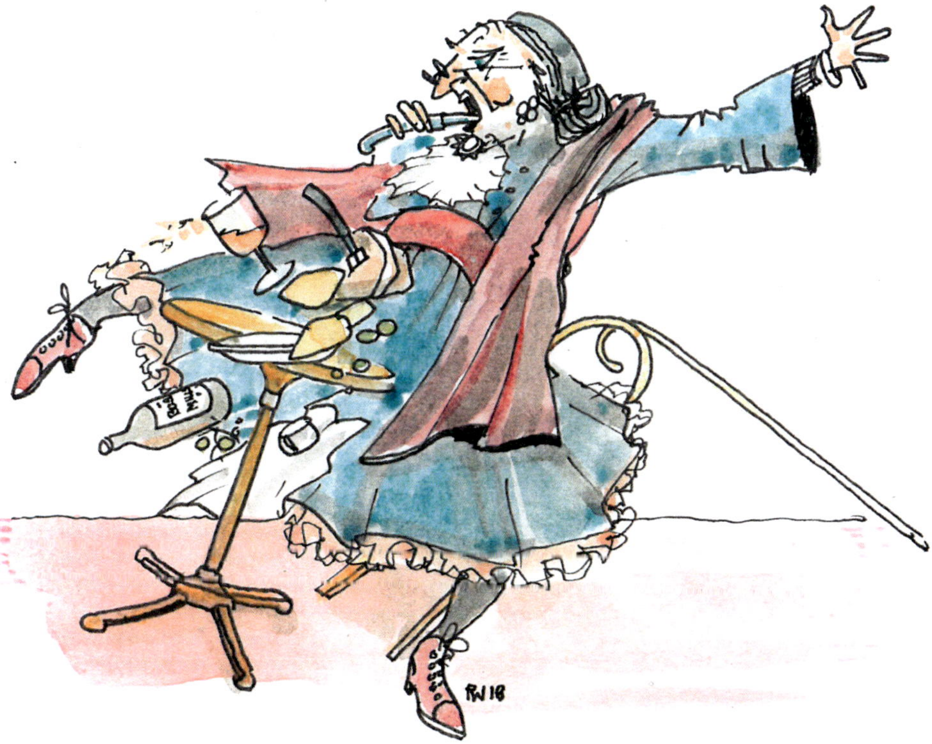
RW 18

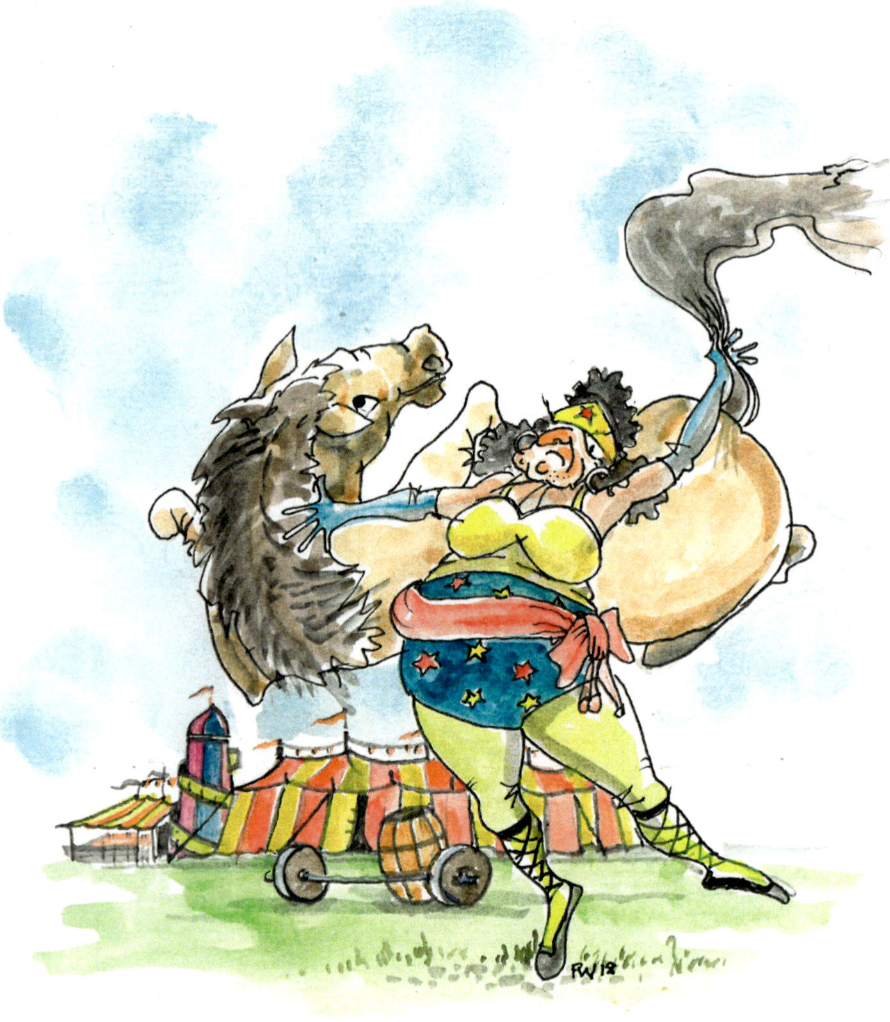
RW18

There was a strong old lady from Kinsale

whose every wager did fail.

Enraged by the outcome,

'twixt finger and thumb

she'd swing the horse by the tail.

Limerick 28

There was a bright young lad from Skibbereen

who built a model submarine.

But on its first trip

his fingers did slip

and he torpedoed the harbour canteen.

Limerick 29

CANT
TEA
BOOM!
ENTS
DESSERTS
BOMBE SURPRISE
RICE PUDDING
TITANIC II

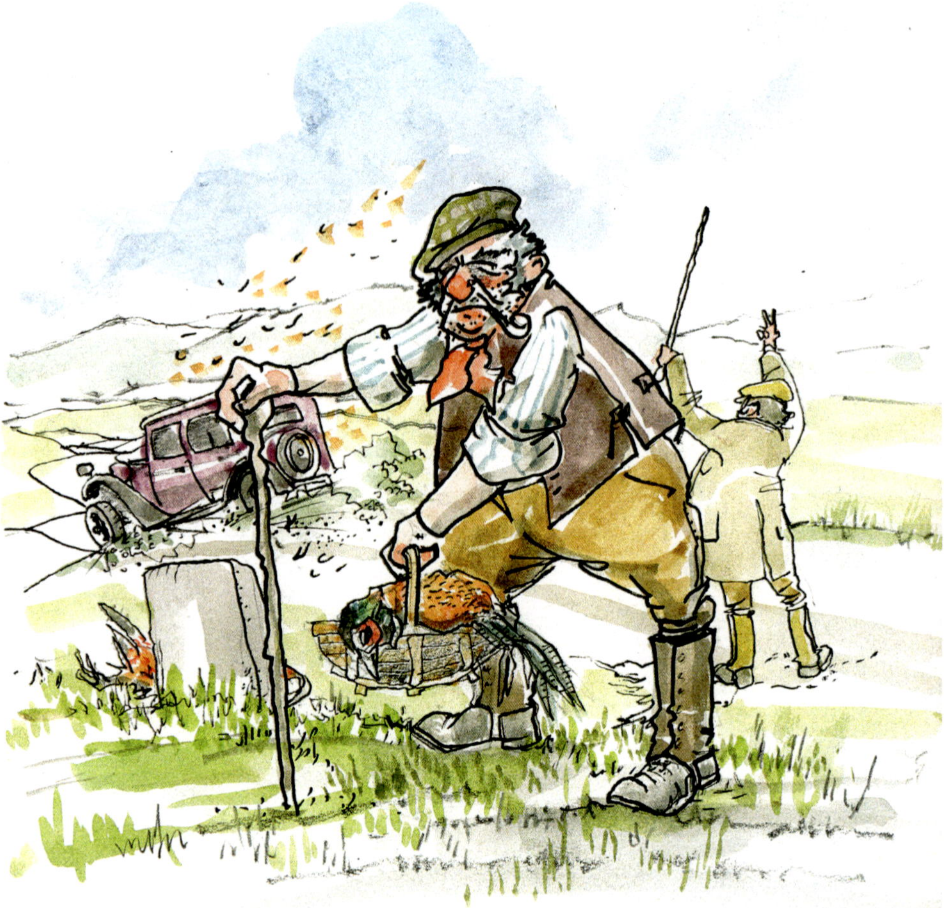

A hairy old man from Skibbereen

was always incredibly mean.

His idea of a present

was road-killed pheasant

he never bothered to clean.

Limerick 30

ABOUT THE AUTHOR

Fergus Dignan is a retired medical doctor. Both of his parents were Irish: his father, Albert, was born in Dublin and his mother in Cork. Sadly, Albert developed dementia and was admitted to a nursing home. On one of his visits Fergus told him a limerick and so much did Albert enjoy it, that Fergus made up some more and continued to recite them to him at each visit. After Albert died, Fergus decided to write a book of these limericks, with some additional ones.

ABOUT THE CARTOONIST

Peter Westley retired from education in 1993. His interest in cartooning and caricatures was inspired, as a young boy, by the humour, observation and technical mastery of Carl Giles. After retirement he developed this interest and also water colours and acrylics. He has no formal art background and is self-taught.